The Pout-Pout Fish and the Mad, Mad Day

Deborah Diesen

Pictures by **Dan Hanna**

Farrar Straus Giroux
New York

MACHOO POOCHY
(official souvenir)

For anyone who has ever felt mad —D.D.

For Jennifer, my wife
And companion in life
Who in wonderful ways
Soothes my mad, mad days —D.H.

Farrar Straus Giroux Books for Young Readers
An imprint of Macmillan Publishing Group, LLC
120 Broadway, New York, NY 10271

mackids.com • Copyright © 2021 by Deborah Diesen • All rights reserved. • Color separations by Embassy Graphics
Printed in China by RR Donnelley Asia Printing Solutions Ltd., Dongguan City, Guangdong Province
Designed by Aram Kim • First edition, 2021 • 10 9 8 7 6 5 4 3 2 1

Library of Congress Cataloging-in-Publication Data

Names: Diesen, Deborah, author. | Hanna, Dan, illustrator.
Title: The pout-pout fish and the mad, mad day / Deborah Diesen ; pictures by Dan Hanna.
Description: First edition. | New York : Farrar Straus Giroux Books for
    Young Readers, an imprint of Macmillan Children's Publishing Group, LLC,
    2021. | Audience: Ages 3-6. | Audience: Grades K-1. | Summary: With the
    help of his friends, Mr. Fish is able to overcome his anger.
Identifiers: LCCN 2020000801 | ISBN 9780374309350 (hardback)
Subjects: CYAC: Stories in rhyme. | Fishes—Fiction. | Anger—Fiction. |
    Marine animals—Fiction.
Classification: LCC PZ8.3.D565 Pok 2021 | DDC [E]—dc23
LC record available at https://lccn.loc.gov/2020000801

Our books may be purchased in bulk for
promotional, educational, or business use.
Please contact your local bookseller
or the Macmillan Corporate and
Premium Sales Department at
(800) 221-7945 ext. 5442 or by email at
MacmillanSpecialMarkets@macmillan.com.

Ant Farm

CYCLO-PUS

The Eyes of the ABYSS

IT Came from Above

Mr. Fish was left with pieces
That he tried to reassemble.

The first thing that happened
On that mad, mad morning
Was a broken favorite souvenir—
It shattered without warning!

BUMP

CRACK

MACHOO POOCHY
(official souvenir)

But his glue stick was *missing*!
His pout began to tremble.

He went to tell his friends,
But they didn't seem to care.
He thought they were *ignoring* him!
He felt his temper flare.

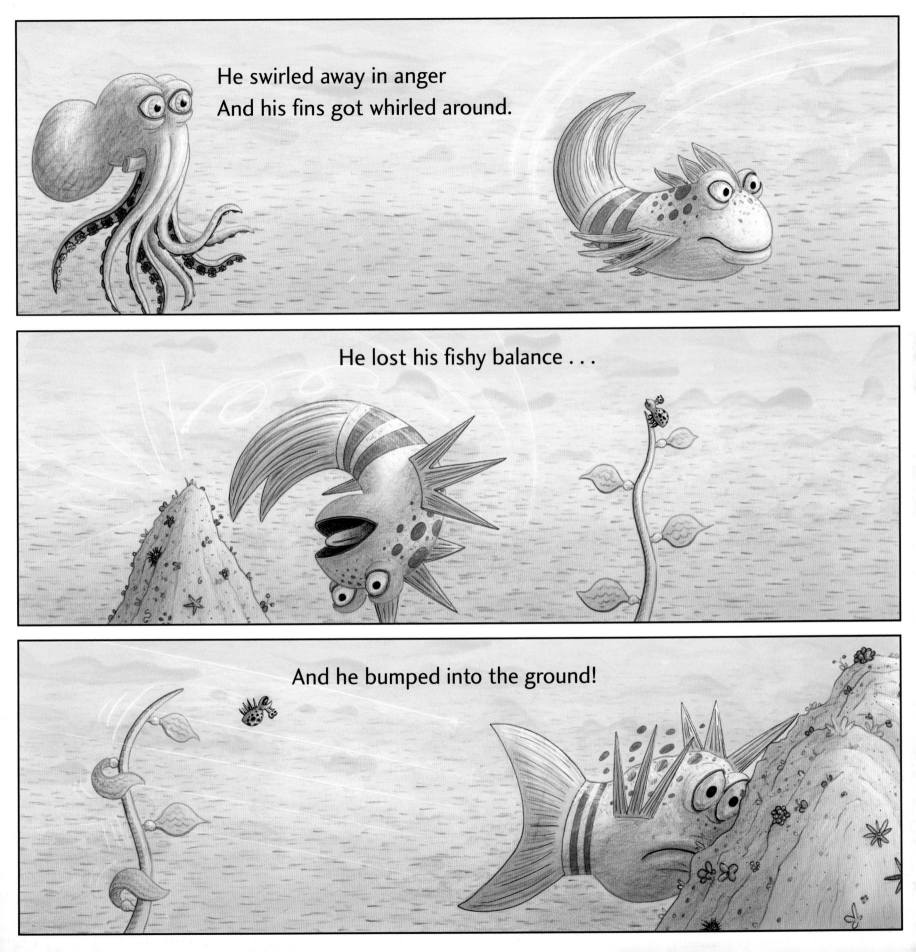

He swirled away in anger
And his fins got whirled around.

He lost his fishy balance . . .

And he bumped into the ground!

He tangled with some seaweed
As he tried to swim away.
He splashed and thrashed and crashed about,
His thoughts in disarray.

MR.
FISH

A feeling filled his gills,
And a sound began to stir.

Much bigger than a blub,
It was a mad,

mad . . .

"GRRRRRRRRRRRRRRRR!"

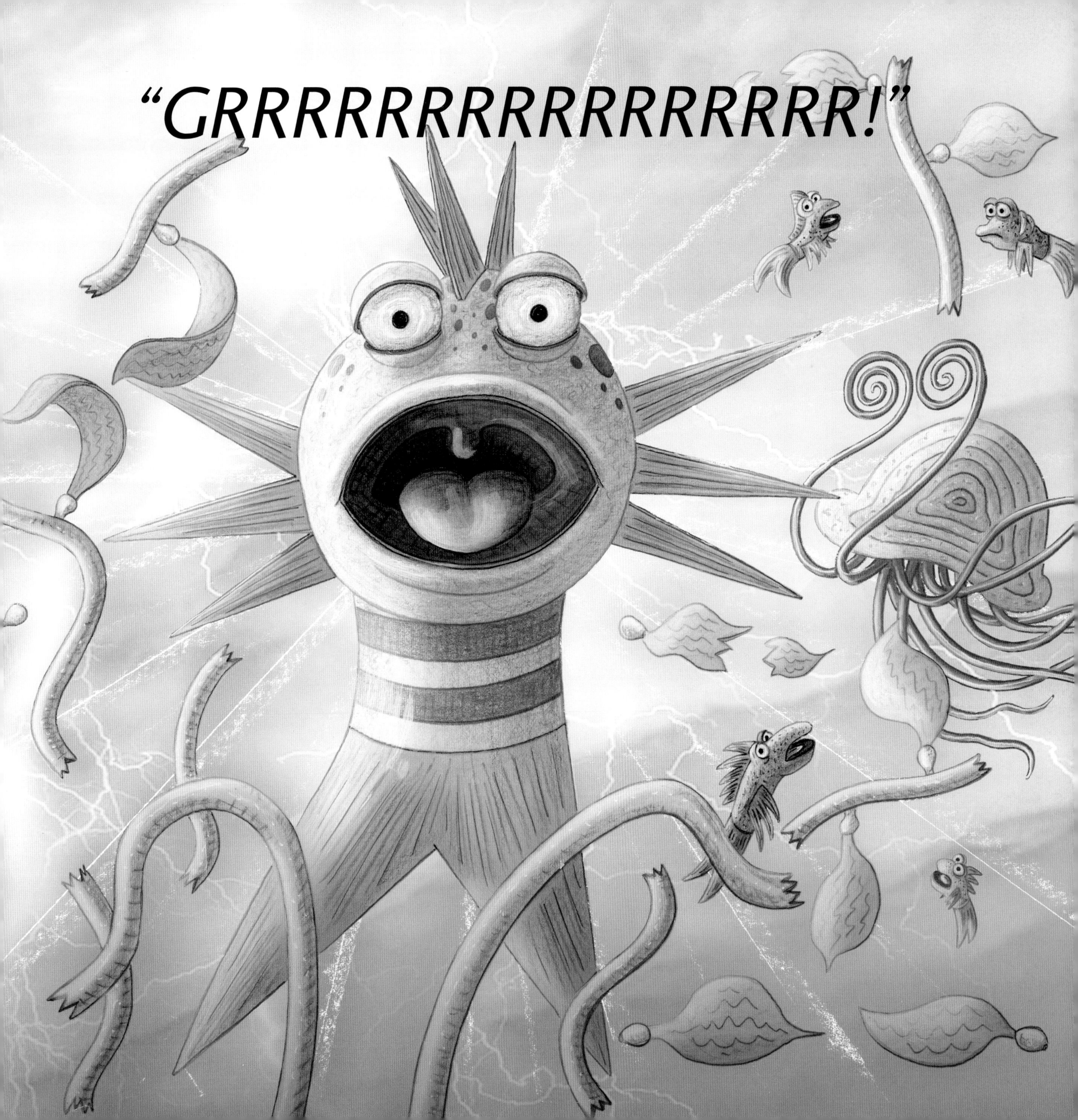

Alarmed, his friends came over,
And they gathered by his side.
"What's *wrong*?" they asked him worriedly.
With effort, he replied.

"It's been *one* thing, then *another*,
Then *another* stacked on top.
I am mad and getting madder,
And I don't know how to stop!"

Ms. Clam consoled her fuming friend.
"We've *all* at times been mad.
It's a challenging emotion,
But it doesn't mean you're bad."

"She's right," said Mr. Jelly,
"And there's much that you can do
To restore your inner balance
And return to feeling *you*."

Mr. Fish said, "Weren't you listening?!
I AM ANGRY TO THE BRIM!"
He scowled and turned away from them,
His *mad* in charge of *him*.

"It's been *one* thing, then *another*,
Then *another* stacked on top.
My mad keeps getting bigger,
And there's no way it will stop!"

Mrs. Squid replied, "You've got this.
To get started, simply *breathe*.
Then slowly count from one to ten
To counteract the seethe."

Mr. Fish was not persuaded,
But reluctantly he tried.
A long breath, and counting, too—
It soothed him deep inside.

He felt a little better,
And he wasn't quite as ruffled.
"But there's still *grrrrr* inside me!"
Mr. Fish's thoughts kerfuffled.

It'd been *one* thing, then *another*,
Then *another* stacked on top.
All that mad had made a muddle.
Could he really make it stop?

MR.
FISH

WELCOME

Mr. Lantern shone his light.
"When you're hurt or feeling sad,
Disappointed, scared, or worried,
Those can channel into *mad*."

MR. FISH MACHOO POOCHY POETRY CONTEST WINNER!

POSTAL SERVICE

MR. FISH

"The solution," said Miss Shimmer,
"Is to talk about what's wrong.
Pick *words* for what you're feeling.
When you use them, you are strong."

WELCOME

"It's too hard!" said Mr. Fish,
With his voice close to despair.
But he breathed again—*in, out*—
And then began to share.

He shared *one* thing, then *another*,
Then *another* stacked on top.
His load began to lighten.
His mad began to stop.

His friends all listened closely
As he spoke about his morning.

MACHOO POOCHY
(official souvenir)

He reflected on the feelings
That were anger's early warning.

He talked about the troubles
That had made his angry mix.
They changed with calm attention
Into problems he could fix.

"It takes one thing, then another,
Then another stacked on top,
But with words and self-compassion
I bring anger to a stop."

Glue
Stick

Maybe S

Not Sure
what this
stuff is

The Pout-Pout Fish had faced his mad,
And look! "The missing glue!"
The pieces are *together* . . .
Mr. Fish feels good as new.

Glue
Stick

MACHOO POOCHY
(official souvenir)